YOSEF'S GIFT OF MANY COLORS

～ AN EASTER STORY ～

BY CASSANDRE MAXWELL

Augsburg
MINNEAPOLIS

YOSEF'S GIFT OF MANY COLORS
An Easter Story

Copyright © 1993 Augsburg Fortress

Cover design: Hedstrom/Blessing, Inc.

Library of Congress Cataloging-in-Publication Data

Maxwell, Cassandre.
    Yosef's gift of many colors : an Easter story / by Cassandre
Maxwell.
        p.   cm.
    Summary: His lavishly decorated egg reminds Yosef and the other
villagers of God's love and miracles.
    ISBN 0-8066-2627-5
    [1. Egg decoration—Fiction.   2. Easter eggs—Fiction.
3. Ukraine—Fiction.]   I. Title.
PZ7.M446515Yo   1993
[E.]—dc20   92-44189
                                                                CIP
                                                                 AC

The paper used in this publication meets the minimum requirements of American National Standard for Information Sciences—Permanence of Paper for Printed Library Materials, ANSI Z329.48-1984. ∞™

Manufactured in the U.S.A.   AF 9-2627

97   96   95   94   93   1   2   3   4   5   6   7   8   9   10

To *My* Christy

The author wishes to acknowledge Lois Paul of the
Chester County Library for her help in researching
the customs and art of the Ukrainian people.

It was early spring in
Ukraine. In the valleys the rich,
black earth was muddy from melting
ice. In the woodlands the scent of wildflowers had
begun to drift on the wind, while here and there a
daffodil added its welcome color to the waking
world. High in the trees a squirrel ate and scolded.

Through the chilly mist of early morning, Yosef walked
toward home, his boots soaked with dew. He was a poor man
and he was facing another long day of hard work. Yet he
whistled at the birds as they began to stir. And he sang songs
of praise to God.

Oh, it was true, he didn't have a new coat or many rubles
to jingle in his pocket, but he was thankful for what he did
have, and he was excited by something he had heard in the
village. He turned an idea over and over in his mind.

"Marusha! Kristye! I am home, dear ones!" Yosef called as he reached his house.

He kissed his wife and lifted Kristye high in the air.

"Papa! Why are you so happy today?" asked Kristye, catching her father's excitement.

Yosef's eyes began to dance as he eagerly explained: "It was all the talk in the village this morning. Each family is to make a special gift and bring it to the church on Good Friday. Then each Papa will present it at the service. It will be as if we are presenting ourselves and all that we are to God."

He glanced at Kristye to make sure she understood.

"Petrovich is bringing a design woven from the wheat he grows. He told me so. Petya is bringing something made out of leather from his cows. But our gift, my dear family," Yosef said with a flourish, "will be the best one of all!"

"The best one?" asked Kristye. "I don't understand. We don't have large wheat fields, and our cow gives milk, not leather."

Yosef laughed. "You are right, little one. We are not wealthy or blessed with much land, but our chickens lay eggs as fresh as any. Our bees make golden honey and fine wax, and our garden yielded good crops last year.

"After supper tonight you will see what your Papa will make. You will see and you will be proud of him! But you have a part in the plan too. You must find the biggest, freshest egg our chickens can lay and you must bring it to the table tonight. Will you do that?" Yosef asked.

"Of course, Papa!" Kristye replied.

Once again Yosef lifted her high in his arms. Then he kissed Marusha's cheek and went out to begin the work of the day. He dug in his little plot, readying the fertile soil for spring seed. He cut more wood. He fed his animals. And he thought about his plan.

Marusha baked bread. She washed clothes and dishes. She embroidered designs on the shirts she had sewn. And she wondered just what her husband was thinking.

Kristye, too, was busy. She made her bed and swept the floor. She shelled corn for the chickens and helped her mother grind coffee. She did not know what Papa was planning to do with an egg, but she was sure that whatever his plan, it would be perfect.

At last it was time to gather the eggs. Kristye scattered the corn, and as the hungry hens pecked at the feast, she carefully examined each egg.

That night after supper dishes were dried and put away, Kristye presented her treasure to Yosef. Slowly, he rolled the large smooth egg over in his fingers. He touched his daughter's cheek.

"It is perfect!" he said.

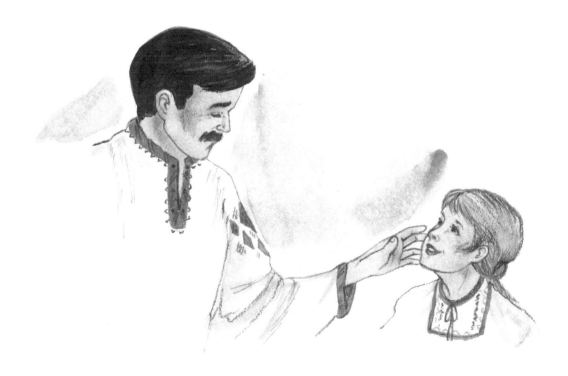

From a box on the windowsill Yosef took a cake of beeswax and a little metal tool with a wooden handle. He put a candle firmly in a tin holder.

Then he carefully drew some lines on the egg with a piece of charcoal. After Marusha and Kristye had admired his steady hand and straight lines, Yosef lighted the candle. He picked up the little metal tool with the wooden handle and held it over the flame. When he was sure the metal point was hot, he pressed it hard into the soft wax. In a moment the wax was liquid and black. With great care, Yosef went over each of his charcoal lines with the wax.

He drew a chicken. "Because our chickens gave us this fine egg," he said.

He drew little sprigs of evergreen. "Because our woods are full of evergreens, and their wood has made our home."

He drew a big star. "For the twinkle in my family's eyes," he whispered.

It was past Kristye's bedtime when Yosef finally held the egg at arm's length to look at it.

Kristye could hardly believe an egg could look so lovely.

"You're right, Papa," she said as he bent to kiss her goodnight. "Our gift will be the best."

The next morning as the sun rose in the sky, Yosef told his family, "Last night, while you were asleep, I thought more about our egg. Why don't we color it?"

"You are so clever, Papa," said Kristye. "Could we make some dye today, Mama?" she asked.

Marusha promised to boil down the dried marigolds left over from last summer's blooms and make yellow dye.

By midday the coloring was cool and ready. Yosef carefully unwrapped the egg. Then he placed **it** on a spoon and slowly lowered it into the dye. A few minutes later, he lifted it out for inspection.

"Oh, Papa," Kristye said, clapping her hands, "it *is* better now."

"Yes," Yosef agreed happily, "I believe it is."

Daylight was fading as Kristye gathered carrots from the root cellar. She helped Marusha chop them so her mother could make stew for supper. By the time she was done chopping, her fingers were orange.

When Yosef came in and saw her fingers, he said, "Hmmm, perhaps our egg should be orange instead. Our carrots *are* the sweetest in the village."

Marusha winked at her husband and put the carrot peelings into a pot. She poured water over them and set them to simmer.

After supper she put the pot of dye outside to cool. Yosef seated himself at the table and once again lit the candle and heated the wax. He covered over some of the designs and drew others.

He made rows of little triangles. "For our carrots," he explained.

Then he lowered the egg into the dye. After a few moments he lifted it out.

"What do you think now?" asked Yosef.

"Beautiful!" was his family's reply.

The next day, each time Kristye passed the table she stopped to admire the egg. There were swirls and checkerboards and other fancy designs. Surely no one else would present a gift as wonderful as this one!

That evening, Marusha made a steaming pot of borscht for dinner. When Yosef lifted the lid to taste the soup, he exclaimed, "The beets! I forgot about the beets! Last year our beets were the biggest in all Ukraine. I should have made the egg red!"

"It's not too late," replied Marusha softly. "I'll boil some beets and make more dye." She patted her husband's hand.

When Kristye went to bed that night, Papa was still seated at the table in the candlelight, working with the little tool. She knew he would be working for a long time, covering over some of the designs and adding some more. She was anxious for morning to come so she could see what the egg would look like.

The next day was Thursday. Only one more day and they would carry their family's gift to church.

Kristye wondered what the others would say when they saw the perfect red egg, and heard her Papa explain what all the little pictures meant.

Just then, Yosef burst into the kitchen from planting over by the barn.

"Blackberries!" he exclaimed. "I've never seen them so early. I am sure that no one else has blackberries yet! And last year our blackberry jam was the best in all the world! Let's make the ends of our egg black," he pleaded.

"Oh, Yosef," Marusha said, shaking her head and laughing. "Here, take the basket and pick some. I'll heat the water."

The sun glowed low behind the trees as Yosef began to work on the egg for the last time. A few more lines. A few more circles. Then, holding the egg tenderly in his fingers, he lowered the big round end into the black dye. In a few minutes, he turned the egg over to dip the little end.

But just like that—it was gone!

"Oh, no!" cried Yosef. "I've dropped it! Quick, get a spoon," he called.

Kristye ran to the cupboard. She handed the spoon to Yosef and watched as he fished the egg from the cup. But it was too late. The precious egg was ruined.

For a few minutes no one said anything. Then Kristye put her arms around her father. "Maybe we can take some of the blackberries in the basket," she offered. But it was no use.

"I worked so hard," Yosef said. "I wanted it to be perfect. Now we have nothing to give."

When Yosef and Marusha came to the kitchen the next morning, Kristye was waiting for them.

"I believe we should still take the egg to church today," she said.

"The egg?" asked Yosef. "But it is ruined. The beautiful color and designs are covered up."

"Papa," said Kristye, "don't you see? The egg is like us. We aren't perfect either. But God still wants us to come."

Yosef stood by the window for a long time without speaking. Then he said, "I believe God has given you more wisdom than God gave your Papa."

Quietly, he wrapped the egg.

That evening at the church, Yosef and his family watched all of the other men from their village walk to the front.

Ivan presented a table runner his family had embroidered. Mykola had carved a wooden box. Jaroslav and his family had created some pottery with details showing their sunflowers. There were kilims and even some metal jewelry. It was obvious that each family had put much love and thought into their gifts.

Yosef was the last to go forward. Before he placed the egg on the table he turned to face the people, but his eyes looked only at the floor.

"I wanted my gift to be the best," he said. "I had my daughter choose the best egg. All week I painted on it with beeswax. I dyed it—first yellow, then orange, and then red. I was trying so hard to make it perfect, but then look what happened."

Yosef unwrapped the egg and lifted it up so everyone could see. "I wasn't even going to bring it today, but my daughter said something that made me change my mind. She reminded me that like the egg, we are not perfect. But God still wants us to come. And so, our Father," Yosef said, looking heavenward, "my family and I wish to present this gift to you. Thank you for accepting this gift and for loving and forgiving us."

Then he placed the egg among the other gifts and walked back to his family.

For a little while no sound could be heard in the church. Then the service continued. When the last prayers were said and the service was over, the villagers crowded around Yosef's family and hugged them. "Your gift is the best one, after all," someone said. Everyone agreed.

Saturday was as sunny as a summer day. It was so warm that all traces of winter at last melted away. Kristye didn't even need her coat when she went to feed the chickens. She walked the cow to the stream for a good long drink. On the way back, she wove a little basket from sweet grass and gathered tiny spring wildflowers to fill it.

Marusha wove some ribbons for Kristye to wear in her hair. Then she made a large round *paska* for the Easter centerpiece. It was full of almonds and orange peel, treats reserved for special occasions.

There were bands of orange where the sky touched the treetops, and one bright morning star still shone as the villagers gathered in the church the next day.

"He is risen!"

"He is risen, indeed!" they spoke in one voice.

Then the cloth that covered all the families' gifts was lifted from the table.

"Look!" Yosef cried suddenly, pointing toward the table. "Look at the egg!"

Everyone stared, their mouths wide open. There in the early morning light glistened the most beautiful egg they had ever seen.

"How can it be?" someone wondered.

"It's a miracle!" another cried.

Kristye sat pondering what had taken place. Her eyes moved slowly from the egg to the window and the sun rising on the horizon. A smile crossed her face.

"Don't you see?" said Kristye finally. "After the long, dark winter, God sends us the bright sun and the warm days of spring. It must have been the sun that melted off all the dark wax. Oh, Papa, the egg was not ruined at all!"

Yosef turned to his daughter. "God *has* worked a miracle, as sure as the miracle of new life!" he exclaimed.

As the first warm rays of sunshine filtered through the windows of the village church, the happy family squeezed one another's hands. And in their hearts they gave thanks for the wonderful way God always turns darkness into light, sadness into joy.

Yosef's Gift of Many Colors was inspired by a centuries-old tradition associated with the celebration of Easter in Ukraine. While no one really knows who made the first colorful *pysanka*, as the Ukrainian Easter egg is called, we do know that the art dates back to pre-Christian times. When Christianity came to the region, new meanings were added to symbols that traditionally had been put on eggs. Because the eggs and their symbols were so important to the peasants who lived in Ukraine, early Christian missionaries to the area incorporated the *pysanka* into the Christian belief and used it to bring more people into the church.

In the story Yosef decorates the egg, but in Ukrainian tradition it has been the mothers who make the *pysanka*, and the art has been passed down through generations of women. Usually the eggs were decorated at night while the rest of the household was sleeping. Before doing each egg, a blessing was asked. Sometimes special songs were sung while the work was going on. It took several nights to complete the process, as many eggs were decorated and each egg took several hours to complete. Even today, with modern equipment, the process is a painstaking and lengthy one!

Like the villagers in the story, Ukrainian families for generations have brought gifts to church during Holy Week. The gift is a basket lined with a clean embroidered cloth and filled with symbolic foods, such as *paska* (Easter bread), *krashanky* (solid-colored, hard-boiled eggs), horseradish, sausage or ham or bacon, salt, cheese, butter, and at least one *pysanka*. The foods are covered with another embroidered cloth, and the basket is carried to the church on the Saturday before Easter for the service that begins at midnight. After the service, a lighted candle is stuck in the middle of the *paska* and each basket is blessed. Then the food is taken back home to be shared.

The *pysanka* is but one of many traditions that are part of a Ukrainian Easter. If you are interested in finding out more about Ukrainian customs or about *pysanka* and how to make them, you may want to consult your library. A good book for further reading on the subject is *Ukrainian Easter Eggs and How We Make Them* by Anne Kmit, Loretta L. Luciow, and Luba Perchyshyn (Minneapolis: Ukrainian Gift Shop, 1979).

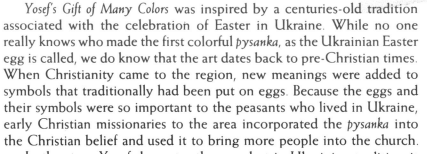